DISNEY
SNEAKERELLA

NOVELIZATION

For information address Disney Press,
1200 Grand Central Avenue, Glendale, California 91201.
Printed in the United States of America

First Paperback Edition, February 2022

1 3 5 7 9 10 8 6 4 2

FAC-025438-22007

Library of Congress Control Number: 2021935114

ISBN 978-1-368-07670-8

For more Disney Press fun, visit www.disneybooks.com

Visit DisneyPlus.com

NOVELIZATION

BY DAVID LIGHT & JOSEPH RASO
AND TAMARA CHESTNA
AND MINDY STERN & GEORGE GORE II
ADAPTED BY SARAH NATHAN

Ｄ𝒊𝒔𝒏𝒆𝒚 PRESS
Los Angeles · New York

CHAPTER
1

NOT ALL FAIRY TALES BEGIN in a land far, far away. This one begins in Queens, New York.

It is home to many kings and queens, although they don't all wear crowns. It is a land of possibility and opportunity—though for many these dreams may feel as far away as a castle in the clouds.

Once upon a pair of sneakers, there lived a special boy who was full of kindness and creativity. He grew up believing in the idea that the perfect pair of kicks could make him fly, make him soar. With his head full of sketches and his heart full of hope, he held tight to these dreams no matter how hard the world around him tried to keep his feet on the ground.

El Morales lived in Astoria, a neighborhood in Queens, New York, just across the river from Manhattan. Queens didn't have shimmering skyscrapers and tall apartment buildings like Manhattan. The streets in Queens were lined with small stores, restaurants, and bakeries with a blend of different cultures and color. El had lived all his seventeen years there, and he loved the neighborhood. His mom had opened a sneaker store called Laces, and they lived above the store in a walk-up apartment. Laces was beloved by everyone, mostly because of El's mom, Rosie. She had a magical way of picking the right sneaker for the right person. Maybe it was in his blood, but ever since he was a little kid, El had been obsessed with sneakers. He had dreams of creating his own sneaker line and was always drawing and thinking about sneakers.

Unfortunately, El's mother got very sick and died. Her sneaker store was now run by El's stepfather, Trey. In the apartment above the store, El lived with his stepfather and stepbrothers, Stacy and Zelly. They were around the same age as El, but that was about the only thing the boys had in common.

El missed his mom and wished his stepfamily understood his passion for designing sneakers. When his mom was alive, she had encouraged him and given him sketchbooks and materials to create unique sneakers.

Things were different now.

El raced down the stairs to the store and climbed into the front window space to put the finishing touches on the window display. He straightened a mannequin's hand to hold a bunch of shoelaces as if the sneakers trailing behind were dogs on leashes. The creative window displays had always been his thing. Lost in his dreams of dancing with his own stylized sneakers, El didn't hear his stepfather calling him.

"El!" Trey called again. His stepfather stuck his head through the small door that opened to the store. "El, you spent enough time on the display." He mumbled to himself, "I've got so much going on right now, I honestly don't know how to get you to focus." He gathered up some papers and boxes around the store. "The shelves need dusting, and straighten up in the back," he said to El. "And clean up the counter with all your mess, please."

"Wait," El said, following him. "Don't I have the day off?"

He looked around at the empty store. Lately, there had hardly been any customers coming in. Since Trey had taken over the ordering, the store didn't stock nearly as many sneakers as it used to. Now there was just one wall of sneakers. Trey was stocking mostly basic shoes and didn't have a sense of what worked for the neighborhood.

The only people in the store were Stacy and Zelly. Stacy was focused, typing on his laptop, and didn't raise his eyes from his screen. Looking like a middle-aged man heading to work, he was dressed in a button-down shirt, khaki pants, and boat shoes. Zelly was wearing his black martial arts uniform and practicing judo in front of a mirror.

"I thought Stacy and Zelly are working today," El said. He shot Stacy a cold, hard look. Why didn't his stepbrothers ever do any work around the store? Why couldn't they help out?

"Yeah, I'm totally booked," Stacy said, pushing his round

wire-frame glasses up on his nose. "I have a Future Venture Capitalists meeting. It's kind of a big deal." He closed his laptop.

"Impressive," Trey said. He turned to El. "See?"

"But I kinda have a thing . . ." El started.

"I'm busy, too," Zelly said, raising his leg up high for a kick.

Crash!

Zelly fell out of his judo pose and knocked over a display of sneaker boxes. "Sorry," he said with a shrug. "I have judo practice."

Trey sighed. "And clean that up, too, El." He put on his coat. "Look, I have an important dinner meeting with a customer tonight. I want to bring him back here after, so this place better be spotless by seven o'clock." He looked straight at El. "No more distractions." He headed out the front door.

"Really?" El said to his stepbrothers. "Sami is waiting for me. I told you I had the sneaker drop today."

"And we told you we have real lives," Stacy said, pushing past him.

"Sorry, dude," Zelly added, slapping El on the shoulder.

El's phone rang, but before he could speak to his best friend, Sami, Trey came back and swiped his phone.

"Bye, Sami," Trey said into the phone before slipping it into his jacket. "No distractions," he repeated to El. His stepbrothers followed their father out of the store, leaving El alone.

Glancing up at the clock on the wall, El realized he might still have time to meet Sami. He threw on a hoodie and paused as he looked at the photo of him and his mom in a frame behind the counter. She would have understood. She would have wanted him to go.

He grabbed his backpack and stuck his head out the front door to see if the coast was clear. When he didn't see Trey or Stacy and Zelly, he flipped the sign on the front door to CLOSED, locked the door, and headed out to meet Sami.

CHAPTER 2

"**H**EY, SAM!! SORRY! SORRY!" El called out when he saw his best friend. She was racing down the alley on her skateboard.

She held up her hands in the air when El ran up to her. "Where have you been? I thought you had the day off work," she said.

El shrugged. "So did I." He jogged next to her as they moved down the street.

"Step-Vader strikes again!" Sami noted. She knew all too well that Trey was not supportive of El's sneaker designs or passion for the newest kicks. Trey was always holding him up at the store, making him clean up or take inventory.

El didn't want to talk about Trey. He quickly changed the subject. "Aren't we gonna be late?" he asked.

"We're already late!" Sami said.

As they raced down the alley, Gustavo, an elderly man in the neighborhood who took care of the flowers in the community gardens, stepped into their path. Gustavo was a good friend of El's and had been a special friend to his mom.

"Whoa!" Gustavo exclaimed as Sami ran into him.

After apologizing for almost knocking him over, El noticed Gustavo was struggling with several large bags of soil. "Need help with this?" El asked. He grabbed two from the man and motioned for Sami to take the other. "Gustavo, I know you are strong, but this is not a one-man job," he kindly told his friend.

Sami shot El a look. They didn't have time to stop and help out in the garden!

"It will just take a second," El said to Sami when he noticed her dismay. He knew they were short on time, but he couldn't pass up helping Gustavo.

"That's a lot of dirt for one guy's tomatoes," Sami said, following El and Gustavo into the garden.

Gustavo smiled. "Well, it's my job to tend to anything around here that needs a little extra love and assistance," he said. His eyes twinkled. "Big or small."

El noticed Gustavo's sneakers. The man had likely had those kicks for years. "I see you rockin' those Tailwinds—crispy," El said. He knew it was a pair of sneakers his mom had helped pick out.

"What can I say?" Gustavo responded, smiling. "They suit me, you think? Your mother always knew exactly what I needed." He reached for the hose and started watering the garden. "She always picked the perfect pair." A sign in the middle of the rose patch said ROSIE'S ROSES. "Why don't you come visit sometime?" he said. "Help me keep her flowers blooming."

El looked around. Gustavo reminded him, "Like Rosie was, we are always here for you."

Sami reached out for El. "We are super late," she said, dragging El to the gate.

Gustavo understood immediately. "It was kind of you to interrupt your plans to help me, El," he said. "Still your mother's son, I see."

"Yes, sir!" El called.

Sami saw the subway train rumble across the elevated bridge. She shot El a pleading look as she ran ahead. She frantically pressed the crosswalk light. "Come on, come on, change!" she urged. They had to make the light to catch the train.

Gustavo looked up and smiled at El and Sami at the corner. With a flick of his hand, he aimed the water from the hose to the street. Mysteriously, the water trailed El and Sami and changed the streetlights as they ran, getting them to the station just as the train arrived.

"Somebody hold the door!" Sami cried, flying up the subway steps.

The two friends slipped into the train just in time.

Gustavo chuckled to himself and then turned the hose back to his flowers.

"We made it!" El said.

"I can't believe you stopped for Gustavo," Sami said. She sat down. "We almost missed this!"

"But we didn't," El said, sinking into his seat.

As the train rattled across the tracks, El noticed a giant billboard announcing the new Adidas sneaker with NBA legend Darius King. The artwork was amazing and bold, and El took in the sight of the updated retro sneaker.

He stood up and pointed the sign out to Sami.

"I hope we get there in time," she said. Sami looked up in awe. "Adidas and King's collab on a rerelease of the 1984 Adidas Forum . . ." Her voice trailed off. The sneakers were a dream!

El and Sami drooled over the cool design. The next billboard was a photo of Darius holding up the new sneaker. The shoe was dropping at King's flagship store in Manhattan, and if they could get there soon, they might score a pair. Getting a sneaker at a drop meant being one of the first to wear a new style, and El and Sami were each committed to being one of the first at King's.

"I can't wait to wear them!" Sami exclaimed.

El pulled a ziplock bag of money out of his pocket. "I got my half," he said. "Did you bring yours?"

The plan was to split the cost of the sneakers and take turns wearing them, a joint venture they had worked out.

"I sold my Air Max 97s to my girlfriend," Sami said, showing her money.

"Which girlfriend?" El said. "You've got like ten!"

Sami smirked. "You've gotta kiss a lotta lady frogs before you find your princess."

El laughed. "Until then, you're stuck with me," he said. He put the money back in his pocket. "At least your kicks are!"

Even though Sami would have to wear extra layers of socks to fit the same size sneaker as El, it was worth it to wear the new King6 kicks. "I don't care if I have to wear twenty pairs of socks to share these kicks with you, as long as I can finally retire these bad boys," she said, raising her dirty white canvas high-tops.

"Here," El said, motioning for her to raise her foot. A smile spread across his face. He had an idea.

Sami shifted her leg so El could work on her sneaker.

She watched as he took his colored pens and sketchbook from his backpack. He sized up her sneaker and then took out a thick black pen. He put a stain of black ink on his finger and made thumbprints all over the sneaker, turning them into a design.

"What did you just do to my sneaker?" Sami asked. She was amazed.

"I was trying to . . ." El felt bad. Maybe Sami didn't like the design.

A smile quickly spread across Sami's face. "Dude, I love it!" she exclaimed. "Do the other one!"

El took a red pen and carefully let ink spill onto his hand. He put a drippy red handprint on the other shoe.

"This is the hottest crime scene I've ever worn," Sami said, smiling. She leaned back and admired her new custom kicks. She took her old-school digital camera out of her backpack and started to take some photos of her newly designed shoes. Turning the camera on El, she captured him sketching a new sneaker design.

"You are very talented," Sami told him. "You know, we could still use this money on materials for you to make us your own pair of sneakers instead." Sami watched El. "Remember the first ones you made in sixth grade? I swear your mom was ready to call Nike."

El shook his head. "C'mon," he said. "You know I don't do that anymore."

"But you could!" Sami exclaimed.

"Sami, you flipped your kicks to get a pair of real sneakers from a legit designer, not your best friend," El said.

"You are a legit designer!" Sami said. She paused and looked at her sneakers. "What makes someone legit, anyway?"

"When was the last time you actually saw me make a pair of sneakers? I just scribble in my notebook," El replied. "That's it."

"That's your stepfather talking, not you," Sami said as she stuffed her camera back into her bag.

"Is he wrong?" El asked. "I'm a stock boy, that's it. And not a very good one at that."

The train stopped, and El slung his backpack on his shoulder. The doors opened, and the two friends sprinted out onto the platform and up the steps to the busy Manhattan street.

As they weaved through the crowd of people, Sami turned to El. "How did you convince the overlord to let you go today?" she asked.

El smiled. "I may or may not have locked up without telling him. . . ."

"Bold!" Sami exclaimed.

"As long as I'm back in time, he won't know the difference," El said, grinning.

The large King6 sneaker flagship store came into view. The store was a sleek modern building with giant windows lining the front and billboard screens on the side. Inside, there were bright lights and tons of sneakers in a range of colors and styles on display. A long line of sneaker fans snaked down the sidewalk, waiting to buy the new King sneakers.

"I think he is gonna know the difference," Sami said, taking in the crowd.

CHAPTER 3

EL AND SAMI WALKED ALONG the outside of the store, looking at all the King6 sneakers on display in the window.

Sami was planning how she would wear their co-owned sneakers first so there would be nothing scuffing up the new kicks. She wanted the pristine pair first. Sami stopped talking when she noticed a girl in front of them was wearing new low-top rubber-midsole sneakers.

"Whoa, hold up," Sami said, staring at the girl's feet. "Where did you get those King6 shoes?" They almost looked like Sleeks, but they weren't high-tops. "Are those player exclusives?" Sami asked.

Before the girl could respond, a guy down the line from them shouted out, "Hey, cutters! The line's back there!" He pointed to the long line of people behind him and stood with his arms across his wide chest.

El and Sami quickly realized that the line didn't end at the corner—it went down two more long blocks.

"I'm never going to make it back to work," El said, sighing. "There are like a thousand people."

The guard ushered the next group of people up in line, and the angry guy moved forward.

"Yo, the line is back there," the guy shouted. "Do I need to come and personally make it clear to you?"

The girl with the cool King6 exclusive sneakers in front of them smiled. She shouted, "Oh, hey, Cuz!" She pulled El and Sami into line next to her. "I'm so glad you found me." She shot the steamed-up guy behind her a look. "I've been waiting for you," she said to El.

El and Sami stared at her as she kept up the act. It took a moment, but they finally caught on.

"Yeah, I've been holding *our* spot this whole time," she said. "We're family."

"This is our cousin," El said to the angry guy behind them.

"Thank you, have a good day," the girl said to the angry guy. She turned and moved forward in line with Sami and El next to her.

"Hey, that was really sweet," Sami said. She faced her savior. "Thanks, uh . . ."

"I'm Kira," the girl said, smiling.

El introduced himself and got lost in Kira's smile. She was wearing a white baseball cap with her tight curls peeking out, and her deep brown eyes were sparkling. He couldn't stop staring at her.

"Hi," Sami said, realizing that El was mesmerized by Kira and forgetting to introduce her. He was definitely into the girl. "My name is Sami. I'm not a part of this . . ." She motioned to the two of them and their puppy-dog looks.

Snapping out of his lock on Kira, El introduced Sami. "That's my friend Sami," he said.

"Hi, Sami," Kira said.

"I just said that," Sami said to El, rolling her eyes. She turned to Kira. "Appreciate the save."

"For sure," Kira said. "That guy was a hypebeast. He deserves to be cut in line, anyway."

"I think he's just really amped up," El said. "I mean, you saw his zebras, right?"

Kira squinted down the line to see the sneakers the guy was wearing. "What do you mean?" she asked.

El leaned in closer to her. "You see how the knit upper is darker just as it meets the boot?" he asked. "It's wet. He probably scrubbed them this morning." He looked back at the guy. "He prepped hard-core for this drop."

Kira shook her head. "I can't believe you noticed that," she said.

"El believes sneakers are a window to the soul," Sami explained. "Kinda like a mood ring."

El shrugged, a little embarrassed. He gave Sami a stern look when she asked him to show Kira.

Sami went on to explain El's talent of being a sneaker psychic. "His mom taught him," she said.

Kira was intrigued. "I have to see this," she said, smiling.

"It's really nothing," El said, trying to downplay the hype.

"I'm sure you aren't really a psychic," Kira said.

El looked at Kira's eyes, and he felt he couldn't say no. He focused on a guy ahead of them who was wearing ultra-clean red, white, and black high-top Jordans. "Okay, check out that guy. He's sporting a classic," he said. "He is thinking if it ain't broke, don't fix it. He's stable, reliable, and has good taste. He gives you Christmas gifts that are actually on your wish list and cash in your birthday card."

"Hmm, not much of a psychic," Kira said. "You could say that about anyone, and how would we know?"

Sami grinned. She liked Kira. The girl wasn't afraid to speak her mind. Sami nudged El. "Kick it up a notch," she said to him.

El looked around at the sneaker fans in line. He focused on a girl to the side with bright blue hair. "Check her out with the pink kicks," he said, nodding toward the girl, who wore classic Chucks with bright blue laces. He predicted that the girl would step on the grate in the sidewalk instead of stepping over it like most people in line. Kira was doubtful. She knew most New Yorkers wouldn't step on those grates. The three of them watched as the girl made her way to the grate—and didn't sidestep it. She stepped right on it, just as El had predicted.

Sami grabbed El's shoulders and shook him. "You are a-mazing!"

"Whoa!" Kira exclaimed. Her eyes were wide with disbelief. "You *are* a sneaker psychic," she said. "Sami, you weren't lying."

El grinned. "You have to pay attention," he said. "People are telling you a story about who they are. That's what the perfect pair of sneakers is. At least what they can be." He paused. "You've gotta give someone a chance to be real."

Kira nodded, taking in what El had said. She motioned to the long line of people waiting to get the new King6 sneaker. "But by your logic, why would all these people line up to wear the same shoe?" she asked coyly.

El had thought about that before and had an answer. "If you put enough of yourself into a design, it's gonna hit," he explained. He studied Kira's face. She seemed to understand what he was saying. "In the end, once I slip that sneaker on, it's my story, right?"

Kira turned and smiled up at El. She had never thought

of sneakers that way—and she liked El's way of thinking.

A guy with a King6 T-shirt stuck his head out of the store and shouted to the crowd. "Sorry, everyone! We're officially sold out of the Forum sneakers for this drop. Thanks for coming!"

A smug shopper walked past them with four shoe bags. He held up the bags for those in line to see his score.

"Did you really need four pairs? You only got two feet," El said as he walked by.

"Was that necessary?" Sami added. She threw her head back, frustrated. "This is the worst day of my life," she moaned.

"This was the most fun I've had talking about kicks in . . . well, ever," Kira confessed. She flashed El a smile.

"Yeah, this is the most fun I've . . . ever . . . with a person . . ." El was stammering and getting more awkward with each word.

Sami stepped forward, trying to save her friend. She pulled Kira's arm. "I think he's trying to say it was nice to meet you," she said.

At that moment, the angry guy from behind them

appeared with a couple of his friends. "I thought you said she was your cousin!" he yelled.

"Um, yeah," El said.

"Very large family. Extended. Lots of cousins," Sami added.

The guy was getting more and more steamed up.

"You know, like a family reunion," Kira said.

The guy and his friends stepped forward.

El took the lead. "Yeah, so I have an idea," he said. He turned to Sami and Kira. "Run!"

CHAPTER
4

EL, SAMI, AND KIRA TOOK OFF down the street with the sneaker goons chasing after them.

Sami threw down her skateboard and taunted the sneaker bully and his friends. She shouted over her shoulder to El and Kira, "I've got wheels! Save yourselves!"

Sami did a couple of jumps and a flip as she narrowly escaped. Kira watched in awe.

El pulled Kira's arm. They couldn't just stand around on the corner. "We gotta move!" he cried. He saw the guys getting frustrated by Sami's escape and knew the goons would be coming for them.

Weaving through the people on the crowded streets, Kira and El made it to the subway station. They flew down the steps to the tracks. A train was arriving as they got to the platform, and when the doors opened, El jumped on. He reached out his hand to Kira. "You up for a little adventure?" he asked.

Kira hesitated and looked back to see the guys coming down the station steps. She jumped on the train just seconds before the doors closed, her white baseball cap flying off, leaving the steamed-up group behind on the platform.

"Adios!" El shouted and waved to the guys through the window.

El and Kira started to laugh as they thought about their escape. Kira looked around the subway car. "Where are we going?"

"Queens!" El said.

It wouldn't be Kira's first trip to Queens. She hadn't been all that impressed by it, but something about El's smile gave her the feeling this visit might be different. Who was this sneaker psychic? She wanted to find out.

The N train rumbled through the tunnel under the East River. Once the train passed through the tunnel, it went aboveground on an elevated track. El smiled at the view out the subway window. He loved that view of his neighborhood.

"You've got more tricks up your sleeve?" Kira asked, eying his smile.

"No tricks," El said happily. "Just home."

El wanted to show Kira his favorite spots in Astoria. There was an energy about Astoria that was different from Manhattan's. He wanted to show her places that meant something to him and showcased Queens's diversity and styles.

"You know," Kira said, "I have been to Queens before."

El watched her smile and his heart beat a little faster. "But you haven't seen it like this," he said.

At the next stop, a group of subway performers got on the train and started dancing. El knew them and joined in the dance. "What time is it?" he called out.

They all answered in unison. "Showtime!"

The guys were amazing, flipping and dancing around the subway car. El wasn't sure what Kira would do, but she got caught up in the rhythm of the music and joined him. They both were dancing and having fun.

The train pulled into El's station, and he led Kira down the station steps to the busy street. "Let's go explore!" El exclaimed.

Kira shrugged. "I'm telling you, I have been to Queens before."

El brushed off her response. Plenty of people visited Astoria, but they didn't really *see* the place. He didn't want Kira to be just a tourist; he wanted her to experience all the sights and tastes of his neighborhood.

As soon as they got to the street, Kira noticed all the little stores and local food shops and restaurants. The buildings were smaller than in Manhattan and mostly made of brick instead of concrete and metal. People on the street greeted El with warm smiles. He seemed to know everyone!

Their first stop was an Italian restaurant. The smells coming from the kitchen were so good! A tall, muscular man, Ernesto, brought a plate out to a small table on the sidewalk. He gave Kira a taste of his famous pesto. Kira thought it was great and was eager to see more. Next El led her to his favorite Indian restaurant. Mrs. Singh, the woman who owned the place, loved El and proudly gave Kira a spoonful of her famous mulligatawny. Kira tasted the soup and nodded. It was delicious! El grinned as Kira approved of the soup. She was enjoying this food tour. She asked for one more thing to truly convince her Astoria was the best place for ethnic food. El knew just the place. Down the block was Aleko's Greek bakery and cafe. Aleko came out to their sidewalk table and presented Kira with his famous dessert, galaktoboureko. He knew Kira would love the sweet treat. One bite of the crispy golden-brown phyllo dough filled with creamy custard, and Kira was a believer.

"Wow," she said. Her eyes were wide. "This really is the best *ever*!"

El grinned. He was so happy to show Kira his neighborhood. As they walked down the street, El and Kira stopped to see three kids playing double Dutch. Kira was impressed with their jump rope skills and enthusiasm. She loved that the kids were hanging out together and having fun.

El grabbed a shopping cart in front of a store and grandly gestured for Kira to hop on. Kira laughed, jumped on the back, and enjoyed the ride. A little farther up the block were the community gardens. El helped Kira out of the cart and led her through the flowers. He bent down and picked a rose for her. El's fingers touched Kira's, and he almost took her hand to hold, but he hesitated and then pulled his hand away quickly.

Gustavo spied El and Kira across the rows of flowers. He chuckled to himself as he put on the sprinklers in the garden to have a little fun. Kira didn't want to get her hair wet and ran to take cover, but El took in the spraying water, leaning back into the sprinkler and laughing. Kira raced back to grab El's hand, and they rushed out of the gardens together.

"Anything else I need to see?" Kira asked, wiping the water from her face. She was beginning to see why El loved this place so much. There was a mix of cultures, energy, and color at every turn. El was right: she had never seen Astoria like this before. This place was the best ever!

El wanted to show Kira one more thing. He spun her around and pointed up. "That!" he exclaimed, pointing to a large graffiti wall across the street. The entire cement side of the building was covered in brightly colored spray-paint art.

"I recognize that!" Kira cried. "I can see that from our apartment."

"Ah, you are a city girl, huh?" El asked. "Well, I bet we can get you a closer look." He headed toward the wall. "Follow me, Manhattan," he said, teasing Kira with the nickname.

El helped Kira climb up a ladder onto a shipping container next to the wall. "Careful," he said.

When El joined her on the container, he grabbed a stray can of spray paint sitting on the ledge. "This wall is always evolving and changing," he said. "Kinda like the city. Everyone gets a chance to express themselves." He held out another can to her. "Now it's your turn."

Kira reached for the paint, but she wasn't sure what to do.

"Just spray whatever you're feeling right now," El said.

He shook his can and sprayed a bright yellow lightning bolt on the wall. "Let's see what you've got, Manhattan," he said, turning to Kira.

Kira shook her paint can. El watched Kira and raised his eyebrows. She had outlined a simple square.

Grinning up at El, Kira leaned into the frame, pulling him in for a selfie.

"I made a frame. If the wall is always changing, I want to make sure I can remember what it looks like right now," she said. She snapped a few selfies with El, capturing their smiling faces.

The afternoon had been picture-perfect.

CHAPTER
5

AS THE SUN BEGAN TO SET, El and Kira sat on a scaffolding platform on top of the container with their feet hanging down next to each other. They looked out on the view. Queens was laid out before them, with the East River and the skyline of Manhattan in the distance.

"You know, my dad grew up in Queens," Kira said. "He talks about his roots a lot, but I can't even remember the last time he set foot around here." She looked down at the colorful streets.

"If he needs a refresh," El said, "apparently I'm also a tour guide."

Kira laughed and told him she would give him a higher tour guide rating if he threw in a sneaker reading.

"Never enough for Manhattan," El joked. "I get it."

Kira laughed again. "Sami said your mom taught you all that," she said. "Is that true?"

"Yeah, she did," El said, looking away. The mention of his mom brought some sadness to the moment. "Before she passed." He took a deep breath. "It's kinda why kicks mean so much to me," he said softly. "It's the only part of her I have left."

"I didn't realize," Kira whispered. "I'm sorry."

El waved her off. "It's okay. I miss her, but every day she's with me," he said. He glanced at the graffiti wall. Then his eyes fell to his feet. "Every time I slip on my kicks," he added.

"That's a pretty cool legacy," Kira replied. "I mean, my family is full of sneaker junkies, but I don't think any of them see kicks the way you do. In fact . . ." She had a thought. She leaned closer to El. "Will you help me with something?"

"For you, Manhattan, anything," El said.

Kira raised her foot. She wanted El to "read" her sneaker. "What do these say about me?"

El hesitated at first, but Kira urged him to tell her what he saw. "Don't go soft on me," she demanded. "I can take it."

He took a deep breath and exhaled. Being honest, he told her the sneakers didn't really say anything. "They're not bad. They are just . . . basic. They are more basic than I would assume from King," he added. "Sorry."

"Are you saying I'm basic?" Kira asked. She leaned back and gave El the side-eye.

El tripped over his words, trying to amend his comment. "I meant a shoe like that could be in fact worn by a person who is basic . . . who is not you. *At all*," he sputtered. "You deserve a one of one."

Kira started to laugh. She understood what he was saying—and more than that, she agreed. "You're right," she told him. El was relieved that she wasn't upset. "And I wasn't worried about that, because I am not basic."

"If you were worried they weren't fresh, why did you cop them?" El pressed her. "Is that, like, a Manhattan thing?"

Kira took the challenge. "It's a life thing," she explained.

"Because sometimes you gotta try something out and hope it surprises. Today I tried out these kicks, and they didn't . . . at all." They both giggled at how true that statement was. "But today I also tried going on an adventure with you, and . . ."

El asked, "Are you surprised?"

"Yeah," Kira said, smiling. She locked eyes with El and felt a connection she had never felt before. "And then some."

There was electricity between them, and they were moving closer and closer to each other. A violinist was playing a romantic tune below on the street corner. Right at the moment when they were about to kiss, Kira's phone rang.

"Ugh, sorry," Kira said. She reached for her phone and saw the screen. "It's my sister. I was supposed to be home by now."

El saw the time on Kira's phone. How was it already seven-thirty? "Oh, no . . . No, no, no!" he cried. He jumped up and started to climb down the ladder.

"What's wrong?" Kira asked.

"I'm deep-fried," El told her as he made his way down to the street. "I gotta go . . . So this was . . ."

"Yeah," Kira said, trying to find the words. "You wanna follow me . . . and I'll follow back?" Then she thought for a moment and added, "Listen, about these Sleeks and how I got them . . . I should tell you—"

El spied a bus moving down the street, and before Kira could say any more, he was racing to the corner stop. "I'm sorry," he shouted over his shoulder. "I have to catch this bus!"

"Hey, wait up!" Kira called. But El was already on the bus. She hadn't gotten to tell him her full name or ask for his. How was she going to find him again? And what would he have said if she had told him that she was Darius King's youngest daughter?

Her phone rang again, and she answered, explaining why she was so late.

Kira threw some money into the violinist's case and turned just as a black town car pulled up to the curb. She reached for the handle to open the car door.

"Your chariot, Miss King," her driver, Roger, said.

"Really, Roger? Tracking my phone?" Kira joked.

"You didn't leave me much choice, the way you ran off this afternoon," Roger said as he drove toward Manhattan. "What am I going to do with you?"

Kira leaned back in the car with her feet out the window. She smiled, smelling the rose El had given her, as the car crossed the Queensboro Bridge.

CHAPTER 6

EL JUMPED OFF THE BUS and ran down the street. Showing Kira around Astoria had been amazing. He had totally forgotten about getting back to Laces before seven o'clock.

He slipped into the dark store and was surprised to see Trey waiting for him. Trey was fuming, his arms tightly crossed over his chest. "Where have you been?" he roared.

"I'm sorry," El said, breathless. "I lost track of time."

"There was no time for you to lose track of," Trey scolded him. "You were supposed to be here, working." He didn't want to hear El's excuses. "I told you I was bringing in someone important tonight," Trey said. He walked around the store. "What did we find? A dark store. A locked door. Totally unimpressive! And totally embarrassing!" Trey stopped in front of the register and held up pages of El's drawings that were scattered on the counter. "This is the real world, El," he went on. "Not some doodles or nonsense you're dreaming about. You gotta get yourself right." He inhaled deeply and threw the papers down. "Honestly, I don't get it," he said. "You weren't disappearing and acting up when your mother was here."

Stacy and Zelly crept down the back steps leading to the apartment. They were enjoying seeing their dad lay into El.

Trey's words hit El hard. His mother had never treated him as a stock boy or looked at his sneaker sketches as nonsense. He pointed to his stepbrothers. "How come you never yell at them when they stick me with a shift?" he asked.

"Don't even," Stacy said, putting his hand up.

"He switches the schedule without even asking," El explained. "He does that all the time."

Stacy turned to his brother. "Zelly, am I the one who locked up and left without telling anyone?" he asked innocently.

"No," Zelly replied, taking the bait for the burn. "That was El."

El wasn't sure why he was in such hot water if his step-brothers were clearly free and able to do whatever needed to be done in the store. "Why don't you tell your dad how you were—"

Trey cut El off. He'd had enough of the bickering boys. "That's enough. El, you are going to take all the shifts next week."

Stacy and Zelly stifled their laughter so their dad wouldn't hear, but El watched their smug faces as they reacted to his punishment.

"It's not fair," El pleaded.

Trey had reached his limit. "Get this place clean. I have more important people coming tomorrow." He stared hard at El. "And until further notice, you're grounded." El tried to respond, but Trey cut him off again. "End. Of. Story."

He turned and went up the steps to their apartment. "Boys, let's go," he said. "El is closing up tonight."

El felt as if he had been slapped in the face. How unfair!

His stepbrothers hung back after Trey went up the stairs. Once they heard the door to their apartment close, Stacy glared at El. "Dude, did we or did we not agree to just stay out of each other's way to make this miserable arrangement tolerable?" he asked.

"That doesn't mean you can shove your shifts on me," El said.

Stacy moved closer to El. "Why are you always complaining?" he asked. "We're the ones who had to leave everything behind in Jersey to move out to this dump."

El felt anger bubbling up inside him. "This place is not a dump," he said, seething.

Stacy jerked his head toward the stockroom. "Are you sure it's not a dump?" he asked. "We just couldn't figure out your system in the back, so it may need some . . . organizing." The smirk on his face was more than El could bear. As Stacy kicked open the stockroom door, El saw the huge mess of boxes the boys had created. The brothers went up the steps to the apartment, laughing at El and his cleanup duties.

El sighed at the mess in the stockroom. He sat down, leaning against the shelving. He thought back to what the store had looked like when his mom was alive . . . when it was just the two of them running the place. Back then, the store had sold only sneakers and everyone had loved the warm, creative vibe to the place. His mom had a way with customers, and her knowledge of what sneakers to sell made the store successful. He remembered how she had loved his window displays and appreciated that he would make scenes with sneakers. His goal was always to get his mom to smile.

And they smiled and laughed often. El remembered lots of fun times in the store with his mom. She was his biggest fan. She'd always help him with sewing and getting a design just right. Thinking about the past, El couldn't shake the memory of his mom getting sick. Those had been dark days. Trey and his stepbrothers were around then, but they didn't dare treat him badly. She was there to protect him.

But then she got even sicker. He remembered the night

Gustavo came and helped Trey hail a cab for his mom. Trey took her to the hospital. She could barely walk and had trouble breathing.

And then she didn't come back. Gustavo had brought his mother's custom sneakers back for El.

El finished sweeping the stockroom and moved into the store. He stopped behind the register and looked at his mom's photo. He wished he could tell her about the girl he had met in line at the King6 sneaker drop that day. He imagined how much his mom would like her, too.

CHAPTER 7

THE BLACK TOWN CAR pulled in front of Kira's high-rise Manhattan apartment building. Kira took another deep inhale of the fresh rose and smiled. Her afternoon in Queens was not what she had expected at all.

She got out of the car, and her doorman rushed to open the building door for her. He warmly greeted the youngest King before she went up to the penthouse apartment.

"Mom? I'm home," Kira called out as the elevator doors opened into the grand apartment.

Kira found her parents and her older sister, Liv, in the dining room. On one wall was a larger-than-life painting of the four Kings; another wall was all glass, looking out on a magnificent nighttime view of Manhattan. Spread across the long dining room table were empty pizza boxes, charts, and thick binders. Clearly, it was a working dinner. Kira leaned against her chair, still holding the rose El had given her. She looked around at her family. "I had the most incredible day!" she exclaimed.

Her mom smiled, noticing the rose and her daughter's expression. "Apparently," she said. "So incredible you completely missed dinner—"

"And all the gala prep!" Liv snapped. She gave her sister a sharp look.

Kira knew that the gala was important to her family and that these meetings were mandatory. She started to tell them about waiting in line at the big drop at the store. She wanted to get to the part where she met El and Sami, but her dad interrupted her.

"Why were you in line?" he asked. "You can just call the office to get you a pair."

Liv looked up. "You were researching the Sleeks, right?"

Before Kira could answer, the conversation was hijacked.

Liv was all puffed up about the hybrid prototype sneakers Kira was wearing. "Low-tops are really trending right now," Liv told them.

"You get me some solid numbers," Darius said, "and I will consider it."

Kira knew SneakerCon was a couple of months away and Liv was trying to get their dad to sign on for something big to boost sales. SneakerCon was a huge deal. Once a year, all the hot designers, big companies, and hard-core fans made the convention a perfect place to launch a new line. Liv was campaigning to showcase the Sleeks low-tops with some hot designer she thought they should collaborate with for a SneakerCon drop. Kira knew there was a tremendous amount of pressure to have the right sneaker for the launch. Sales were down from the year before. The Kings needed a hit.

Kira's mom noted that she was very quiet. She caught Kira's eye. "Something on your mind, Kira?" she asked.

"I don't think the Sleeks are gonna put us back on top," Kira said.

Liv shifted in her seat while her dad pressed Kira for more information.

"They don't say anything," Kira said. She thought about her conversation with El and how he had talked about what a sneaker could say about a person. "There's no story behind them." She turned and faced her dad. "They're not bad. They're just a little . . . basic."

Liv's face hardened. "You did *not* just call me basic," she snapped, insulted.

Kira realized she had her dad's full attention. She chose her words carefully as she tried to explain her thoughts about a new sneaker launch. "I think that we can do better. We are not really tapped into the street all the way up here." She looked out at the penthouse view. "We need a new voice," she said. "Someone fresh."

"I have a pile of research that says differently," Liv said, scoffing. She picked up one of the thick folders in front of her.

"It's just my opinion," Kira said. She was gaining more confidence as she spoke. "Shouldn't my opinion count for something?"

Kira's mom smiled. "It does," she said.

Darius took a moment and pushed back in his chair with his long legs stretched out before him. "Your mother is right," he said. "Problem is something I learned a long time ago: you cannot run a business on your opinions alone. Talent and passion is only part of it. But my team has experience, and they do all this research. If they say Sleeks is what we need right now to put us back on top, that is what we are going to do."

Kira stared at her father. "Dad, just give me a shot," she begged. "You gave Liv a chance when she asked."

Darius softened a little, and his wide smile spread across his face. "I'm really happy that you're getting more involved in the family business," he told her. "But a lot of jobs rely on this decision. You gotta come at me with something other than 'I think they're basic and I'm right.'"

Kira's mother, Denise, jumped in. "You know what? It can't hurt to keep looking," she said, putting a hand on her husband's arm. "We have a little more time."

"All right," Darius said, standing up. Kira smiled—and

Liv nearly exploded. "I don't think you are going to find this person, but I'll let you try."

Kira held her breath as her dad went on. The gala was soon, and finding the "right" designer was going to be tough. Liv was annoyed. She didn't appreciate her little sister's dissing her choice of designers.

"If you find a designer that we should consider," Darius told Kira, "someone who speaks to you, tells a story, and has the experience to back it up, we'll try it out."

Kira grinned and gave her dad a big hug. He was going to let her try!

"The gala is in two weeks," Darius said. "If we haven't found a designer who changes the game for us by then, we'll go with your sister's recommendation."

Denise saw the tension growing between her daughters. She tried to keep the peace and steered the conversation to the gala charity auction.

Darius's phone rang, and he had to take the call. He knew the gala planning would be in good hands without him.

Kira called to her dad. "Thanks," she said.

Darius put his hand up for a mimed dunk shot, which Kira mirrored. It was their own special gesture.

Yeah, she knew someone who could give them a slam dunk.

If only she knew his last name . . .

CHAPTER
8

THE NEXT DAY, El stood in front of the corner newsstand with his mouth agape. Sami had dragged him there to look at the cover of a magazine. Now he was shaking his head in disbelief. "It can't be," he said to Sami.

Sami nodded and reached out to grab the magazine for a closer look. There on the cover of *Big Apple Digest* was the King family, including Kira King.

"You touch it, you buy it!" the newsstand guy scolded Sami. She thought fast and took a photo of the cover with her camera, which was hanging around her neck.

"Hey!" the newsstand guy yelled.

The two friends took off.

"Dude, we were hanging out with Kira King," Sami said as she and El walked toward Laces. "Darius King's daughter. Aka sneaker royalty."

"How did I not know?" El asked. "I've had the King's poster on my wall since I was, like, five!" El looked at the Manhattan skyline. Somewhere in one of those high-rise apartment buildings, Kira was waking up in a penthouse. "That's crazy," El said as they walked into Laces. "She's like a princess."

And then he realized . . .

"Oh, no, Sami," he said, stopping in his tracks. "I messed up!" He put his hand to his head as he remembered what he had said to Kira about her sneakers.

"Don't worry about it," Sami said, heading back to the stockroom. "Like you would know who Kira King is by sight." She walked past Trey and saw the very basic, ugly shoe he was unpacking. She turned, made a face at El, and then turned to the stockroom.

El sighed. Sami didn't understand the gravity of the situation. "I dissed her King6 Sleeks," he whispered, following Sami. "I dissed her father!"

"What were you gonna do?" Sami asked. "Lie to the girl? You have to call it how you see it." She sat down at the desk and switched on the computer while El started to clean up the boxes scattered around the floor. "You're missing the big picture," Sami said as she tapped the keyboard. "Now that we know who she is . . ." She leaned back in the chair triumphantly. *"Boom!"* She moved her seat to the side so El could see the screen. On the monitor was an ad for the King6 Annual Charity Gala. "Now you know how to find her again," Sami said proudly. She smiled up at El. "You're welcome."

El rolled his eyes. "Okay, at the most exclusive sneaker event of the year?" He clapped his hands. "Great idea," he said sarcastically. He shook his head. "It's not gonna happen."

"How is this not, like, the definition of fate?" Sami asked. "Come on! You like her, she likes you . . ." Sami teased him.

El backed away. "You don't know that," he said.

"Yeah, okay," Sami said. "I was sweating from the heat between you two yesterday." Sami uploaded the picture of the magazine cover she had taken at the newsstand and zoomed in on Kira's face. Making kissy faces, she leaned into the screen as El stood behind her, blushing.

El folded his arms across his chest. "You said you saw . . . like, heat?" he asked.

"Just a little bit," Sami joked. Then she grew serious. "Dude, take a shot."

"Never gonna happen," El said. "It's not scientifically possible."

He was a nobody—and Kira, well, she was a total somebody.

"If you say you are just a stock boy . . ." Sami threatened.

El shoved some boxes on the shelf in front of him. "I was going to say a nobody," he said.

"You want to show her you're a somebody?" Sami asked. "Show off your talent. Design some sick kicks for the gala!"

The gala was in two weeks. How was he going to whip up something in time?

"This is your shot to show Miss Kira King who you really are," Sami told him. "Come on."

Trey yelled for El from the front of the store, bringing him back to reality. He didn't have time to design sneakers and go to charity galas. He had to stack boxes and clean up. "Coming!" he called. Then, to Sami, he said, "Never gonna happen."

Sami called after him, "Hey, never say never!"

When El walked into the front of the store, he saw Mrs. Singh sitting in a chair, with Trey kneeling in front of her. There were several boxes around her feet. El could see Trey was showing her some fancy Italian leather loafers. He knew Mrs. Singh was not interested in the high price tag.

"El!" Mrs. Singh called out. Her face lit up when she saw him. She stood and gave him a loving hug. Then she reached into her bag. "I've been meaning to drop these off just in case your allergies acted up this fall. Your mom always swore by my home remedies," she said. "So give them a try."

"Okay, I will," El said, taking the bottle.

Mrs. Singh patted El softly on the cheek. She turned to leave but stopped to look over her shoulder at the new window display El had been working on. In the center of the window was a large clock with sneakers in place of the numbers. She gushed over the display and added, "Rosie would love it."

El appreciated Mrs. Singh's compliment and was happy that she thought his mom would approve.

"Think about what I said, Mrs. Singh," Trey called after her. "I'd be happy to throw in a free pair of Odor-Eaters!"

Mrs. Singh paused with her hand on the door. She whispered to El, "Did he just say my feet stink?"

El nodded and waved her off. When El closed the door, Trey turned off the charm. "I don't get this neighborhood. They all pretend to be one big happy family, but when it comes down to it, where are they?" he barked. He had tried to bring in new styles and different types of shoes to make the store more successful, but so far sales had been really slow.

Trey had no idea what people in the community wanted. The new inventory he was stocking was not appealing to anyone.

"Well, it looks like this shop is going back to the sneaker business anyway," Trey said. He jotted down some notes on his clipboard.

"Really?" El exclaimed. He jumped up and moved closer

to Trey. He couldn't believe his luck. "Maybe I could curate the—"

Trey cut him off. "Yeah, I've spoken to Foot Locker about buying the space."

El froze. Trey's words were ringing in his ears. "You're selling the store?" he asked, shocked.

Trey explained he was a month behind on the mortgage and sales were way down. "El, you got to get your head out of the clouds," he said. "Not everything works out the way you want it to."

"You think I don't know that?" El spat. There was so much pain in his heart he thought he would burst. He looked at the photo of his mom. "Mom wouldn't want you to sell." He paused. "If you ever loved her—"

Trey slammed his hand on the counter. "I did love her!" he yelled. "You think this is something I wanted to do alone?" His head dropped. He looked around the store. "Enough is enough. Sometimes you just gotta let dreams go."

El stared at Trey. It was rare that his stepfather showed any emotions.

"This was me and your mother's dream, too." Trey turned and went up the steps to the apartment. His words hung in the air.

When El returned to the stockroom, he found Sami still sitting at the computer. She was scheming a way into the King6 gala. She had found out that someone's best friend, Jeremy, and his cousin were working as waiters at the gala and could get them catering uniforms. If Sami and El got there before the event started, they could sneak through the service entrance. Then, once inside, they would change into gala wear and blend in as guests. Sami grinned. Even she was impressed with the plan she had come up with for El to meet up with Kira again. When she saw El's reaction, she thought he was concerned about dressing as waitstaff. "It's fine, we can costume change there," she told him.

El looked off into the long rows of shelving. "Trey is selling Laces," he said slowly.

"He can't do that, can he?" Sami asked.

"He just did," El said. "The thing my mom loved the most is gone." The reality of his words hit El, and he sank to the floor.

"That's not true," Sami told him. She walked to him. "You're still here, and as long as you carry on her legacy, she's not fully gone, either."

El looked around the messy stockroom. "I don't know how to do that without this place," he said softly. "This place was everything to her."

"It's just a place, El," Sami said. She of all people knew how much Laces meant to El. The store meant something to her, too. She had grown up there and learned how to tie her laces ten different ways. "You don't have less of your mom because the store is gone," she added. She watched El's face. She knew how painful selling the store would be for him. "I think we both know what she'd want you to do," she said. "Get up!"

Sami extended her hand to El. "Come on, you've got sneakers to make."

El knew Sami was right. After he finished cleaning up, he flipped the store sign on the front door to CLOSED. He lifted the shelf under the staircase and saw the tiny keyhole. He reached for the key on the chain he was wearing around his neck and turned it in the lock. The door opened to a hidden work space. El switched on the lamp. He hadn't been inside in ages. There was a sewing machine covered in cobwebs, scraps of materials, and a bunch of sneaker sketches on a table. Up on a shelf was the first pair of sneakers El had ever made. He smiled as he opened a box filled with his old sketches of sneakers. He remembered his mother's advice: *See the person; then you'll see the shoe.*

Fired up with determination, El sat down with his sketch pad to create a new sneaker. He thought of the scenes around Queens, the graffiti mural wall, the shops, and the people. First he used the computer to render a 3D model of his creation, and then he turned to his sewing machine. He took pieces of leather and carefully stitched up the shoe. He added emblems that represented his neighborhood. When the top part of the sneaker was done, El went to Mr. Brown's mold and casting shop down the street from Laces. He brought bags of recycling and melted down the plastic for the shoe soles. The clear sole was perfect for the look of the sneaker. He even found a mini Queensboro bridge from Kwon's miniature store. He slipped the tiny model into the sole of the sneaker. Now he was nearly done, but there was one more important detail.

El took his mother's old sneakers and touched the red rose-shaped patch sewn into the fabric. He paused and then ripped the rose off. He was going to make this sneaker the best he could—with his whole heart.

CHAPTER 9

EL STOOD OVER THE STOVE in his family's small apartment kitchen. He dished out food and carried the plates into the dining room. He, as usual, had made dinner for his stepbrothers and Trey.

Zelly looked up when El walked into the room. "This is whole grain, right?" he asked, looking at the toast on the plate El was holding.

"Yeah," El barely responded. His eyes were on Trey's empty seat. When Stacy said Trey was out for the night with the Foot Locker rep, El tried not to show his excitement. He simply nodded. He had spent the last two weeks working hard on his one of ones for the King6 gala. With Trey already gone for the evening, slipping out of the apartment to go to the event would be much easier. Maybe Sami's crazy plan to get into the party would work. He hoped his stepbrothers would be out for the night, too.

El casually asked his stepbrothers about their evening plans. Zelly excitedly shared that he was going to a judo exhibition, but Stacy sensed El was up to something. Stacy put his fork down and gave El a long, hard look.

"I'm just gonna finish up the inventory for the week," El told them. "You know, make up for the other day." El saw Stacy was skeptical. "Just leave your dishes," he said with a smile. "I'll do them later." He was trying to act as casual as possible and headed out the door. "Have fun at your . . . thing."

Stacy watched El slip out and turned to Zelly. "That seem odd to you?" he asked.

Zelly leaned back in his chair. "Yeah," he said.

Stacy shoved his seat away from the table. El was up to something, and Stacy wanted to know what. He motioned for Zelly to follow him down the steps to the store. Stacy flipped on the lights and saw El in his catering outfit with his backpack slung over his shoulder, heading to the front door.

El dropped his phone when he saw Stacy and Zelly.

"Inventory is the other way," Stacy said, giving El a cold stare.

"Yeah," El said, trying to cover his attempted escape. He struggled to be cool. "I was just checking the door to make sure it's locked." He reached for the knob. "And okay, it is," he said quickly. "So I'm just gonna go back there and do my work."

Both Zelly and Stacy knew El was lying. They grabbed El's backpack straps and held him back. Stacy took El's phone and put it on the counter.

"Give me my phone back," El demanded.

Stacy ignored him. "Just because Dad's out doesn't mean you're not still grounded," he said.

"Look, I've got to meet someone important tonight," El pleaded. He tried to level with them. Maybe if he was honest, he could get them to let him go.

Stacy nodded to Zelly. Time to set their own plan into

action. They dragged El and tossed him into the stockroom, then closed and locked the heavy doors.

El scrambled to the door and called out, pleading for them to open it. He had to get to that gala! El turned and ran to the back of the stockroom, to the metal grate door. He figured he could escape out the back of the store. But Zelly and Stacy had already gone around back and were waiting for him.

"I don't know where you're going," Stacy said to El, "but we're this close to Dad getting us out of here. And you're not going to ruin it for us!" He closed the metal grate door and locked it.

And then the brothers were gone.

El banged on the door. "Come on, guys!" he yelled. "Let me out. I have somewhere to be!"

When there was no response, El slumped down to the floor and pulled his knees up to his chest. Sami was probably frantically texting him, wondering why he was so late. He thought of his phone sitting on the counter where Stacy had put it. If only he could contact Sami . . . Their sneaking into the King gala was definitely not happening while he was locked up in the stockroom.

El put his head in his arms. He couldn't believe he was stuck. After all the arrangements Sami had managed to make and all the time he'd spent creating his sneakers, he wasn't going to get to the gala. He'd had a chance to see Kira again, and now he was locked in the stockroom. Some stock boy he was.

He banged his head against the bookcase behind him. Tacked on the side of the bookcase was an old picture of a sneaker El had drawn. Magically, the lines of the drawing fell from the page and took flight. Like tiny birds, the lines flew out of the locked stockroom through the metal grate door and down the street.

Suddenly, there was a clicking sound and then a loud snap.

The door flew open.

"Gustavo!" El cried. "What are you doing here?"

He jumped up and gave the old man a huge hug.

CHAPTER
10

GUSTAVO **STEPPED INTO** the stockroom and grinned. "Seems like you are in need of a little assistance," he said, his eyes sparkling. "Don't you have somewhere to be? Come on. Let's go!"

El followed Gustavo outside and spotted Sami running down the street.

"El!" Sami shouted, racing toward him. "Where have you been?" When she reached him, she saw Gustavo. "What's he doing here?" she asked.

"A little faith, Sami," Gustavo said. He turned to El. "If you're gonna make this happen, you need the most important ingredient." He motioned to El's backpack. "The whole neighborhood is talking about your sneakers."

El pulled out the sneakers he had made for the gala. They were an amazing patchwork, paying tribute to Queens and all the things that meant something to El—especially the roses from his mom's sneakers. He slipped them on.

"Whoa!" Sami exclaimed. Her eyes grew large as she took in the unbelievable design. "Those are incredible," she said, totally in awe.

"Are you ready for your big night?" Gustavo asked.

El looked at Sami. He knew it was too late to meet up with the catering contact to get into the gala. They had missed their chance to sneak into the party. "I did all this work for nothing," El said, deflated.

"Maybe we can find another way in," Sami offered.

"You put in the work, El," Gustavo said. "Don't give up so easily." He walked up to an old covered car parked across the street and gently waved his hand over it.

Whoosh!

Gustavo peeled the cover back to reveal a beautiful shiny orange vintage car. He tossed Sami the keys.

Sami looked at El: had that fancy car been there before? What was happening?

Just then, a truck rumbled down the street.

Gustavo's eyes sparkled. He kicked a bundle of news-papers into the street so the truck had to swerve. A large box fell out of the back of the truck. Sami ran to the box and pulled out two hangers with suits. She gave one to El and ducked behind a newsstand to change into her outfit.

"This jacket," Sami cooed as she slipped it on, "is every-thing!" The cropped jacket fit Sami perfectly and made her feel gala-ready. She glanced at El. He was wearing a suit that looked as if it had been tailored just for him. He cleaned up *very* nicely.

Gustavo smiled. He had watched El grow up and seen the many thoughtful things he had done for his mom and others in the neighborhood. Ever since Rosie died, Gustavo had continued to keep a special watch over El. He noticed that El was always there to hold a door, help carry in pack-ages, or lend an umbrella in the rain. Gustavo was more than willing to help El out in turn and to spread a little magic.

Now dressed in suitable gala wear, El and Sami got into the vintage orange car. The convertible top opened, and

El and Sami couldn't believe their eyes . . . or their ride! A rose was stuck in the visor on the driver's side, and Gustavo reached over to slide the flower into El's jacket pocket. He gave El a pep talk and some advice.

"All bets are off if you're not home by midnight," Gustavo told him.

El looked at the window display at Laces. The sneaker clock glowed. Gustavo hit the car and propelled it forward.

El and Sami were off to the Manhattan gala to make some magic happen, in a car with the license plate PMPKN XPRS.

CHAPTER
11

THE SOUPED-UP ORANGE CAR sped over the Queensboro Bridge and through the Manhattan streets to the King6 store. In front of the store, there were bright lights and a long red carpet spread over the sidewalk. The press, with cameras and microphones, were photographing and interviewing models and celebrities going into the gala. The scene was like a big-time Hollywood movie premiere.

El parked the car on the street, and he and Sami walked the red carpet into the glamorous store. Sami took a couple of pictures with her camera. She couldn't believe the scene! There were lights and elaborate decorations. The place was full of beautiful people making their way up the long escalators to the party.

Sami spun around. "Let's look for a side entrance," she whispered to El. "Maybe we can still find Jeremy or his cousin—"

Sami was cut off by a security guard waiting at the escalators. "Tickets, please," the man said.

Panic surged through El's body. They didn't have tickets for the party! How were they going to get past the guards?

El looked down, avoiding the guard's glare. He noticed that where Gustavo had placed the pink rose in his jacket pocket, there was now a pair of King6 gala tickets. When El pulled the tickets from his pocket, a few rose petals spilled out. He handed the tickets to Sami, who gave them to the security guard.

"Enjoy your evening," the man said, moving aside so they could ride the escalators to the party.

"We shall," El said, grinning.

El and Sami looked at each other in disbelief as they rode up to the party. Never had they seen anything quite like the scene at King6's. The massive store was decked out with lights, large screens, and tons of food: there were food stations scattered around the store, and waiters were walking around with full trays. Everyone was wearing super-stylish clothes, and the vibe was electric.

"This is next level," Sami said, eyeing all the people decked out in expensive outfits.

"Yeah, this is . . . a lot," El mumbled as he walked through the room. He was intimidated. He couldn't believe all the people. How was he going to find Kira? He pressed on through the dense crowd, searching.

When they passed a waiter holding a tray full of tiny spoons filled with sushi, Sami's eyes lit up. She took a spoon in each hand. "Oh, word!" she exclaimed. "They got spoon appetizers!"

El was focused on finding Kira. Sami told El to go, and she would hang back—with the food. "And don't forget," Sami called out to El before he disappeared into the crowd, "you're a rock star!" She snapped a few pictures of El and his amazing sneakers.

Roberta and Reggie, two industry executives hanging around, took notice of El—and his sneakers. Sami's callout gave them pause. Roberta leaned over to Sami. "Excuse me, who was that?" she asked.

"We need those sneakers," Reggie added.

"We've never seen anything like them," Roberta said.

Sami grinned. "That's 'cause they're one of ones," she said. She reached for another appetizer from a passing waiter's tray and popped it into her mouth. "You can try to convince him to make you a pair, but I've been waiting for years."

Reggie's eyebrows shot up. "He's the designer?"

"Who's he with?" Roberta asked. They moved in closer to Sami.

"He's with me," Sami said, a little confused.

"No, she means who is he with . . . What company?" Reggie asked.

Sami eyed the two executives and then thought better of her response. She tossed her head back. "I'm not at liberty to say," she replied coyly.

Roberta groaned and looked at Reggie. "She's messing with us," Reggie said.

Sami was enjoying playing this role. She was El's best PR agent. She took a baby quiche from a tray and popped it in her mouth. "You sure about that?" she asked before walking away from the two sneaker executives.

Roberta vowed to find out who El was "with" and began moving around the party.

While El continued searching the room for Kira, he didn't notice that people were staring at him—and his sneakers. Everyone in the room was talking about his sneakers and who might be collaborating with this hot new designer.

Kira walked through the crowd wearing a long white sparkling dress and matching King6 high-tops. Her hair and makeup were perfect, and she turned heads as she moved among the guests. She passed a group of people and over-heard them talking about a new designer. The room was buzzing with excitement about a new sneaker collab.

"Apparently, three brands are chasing him and he hasn't committed yet," Roberta said to a group of people.

Kira looked over her shoulder and wondered who the woman was talking about. She turned around, straining to hear more about this new designer, and backed up right into El. As they both turned to see each other, the whole room disappeared. They were in their own bubble, and the crowded party faded away.

"It's you," Kira said. "I was worried I'd never see you again." She paused as she noticed his swanky suit. "Wait, why are you here?"

El looked at her, grinning. "I was . . . hoping to see you."

"Wait!" Her eyes lit up. "This time, I wanna show *you* something." She grabbed El's hand. "Come on."

They zigzagged through the crowd. At the back of the room was a door with a velvet rope in front. A guard stood by and lifted the rope for Kira and El. Kira put her finger to her lips and took El inside the room. El's eyes widened as he saw the display in front of him. He didn't know where to look first. Stretched out before him was a huge showcase of all the classic King6 sneakers. They were displayed on clear shelves that reached to the ceiling and covered every wall in the circular space. Kira watched El and grinned. She could see how mesmerized he was by the display.

"Sneaker heaven!" El exclaimed. He reached out to hug

El worked as a stock boy in a shoe store that used to be owned by his mom. But he had bigger dreams.

El and his best friend, Sami, took the train into Manhattan for a sneaker drop. Their plan was to buy a pair of new sneakers—but that didn't stop El from decorating Sami's old ones on the way.

El and Sami met Kira in line at
the King6 sneaker drop.

El took Kira to his neighborhood garden in
Queens . . . and her feelings for him bloomed.

El and Kira had a real connection. You could say the writing was on the wall. ;-)

Sami knew El had the skill and passion to make amazing sneakers. She just had to convince him to believe in himself.

When El and Sami needed a little magic to help them get to the King6 gala, Gustavo came to their rescue.

El and Kira had only a short time together at the gala before he had to run out when the clock struck midnight.

Kira's parents, Denise and Darius King, held court at their annual charity event.

Fresh kicks! When Kira showed her father the sneaker El had designed—the one he left behind as he ran out of the gala—the King couldn't help being impressed.

When Kira discovered El had been less than truthful about who he was, she was hurt . . . and angry! El tried to explain himself, but she wouldn't hear it.

El's sneaky, spiteful step-brothers, Stacy and Zelly, tried to ruin El's plans to go to SneakerCon and fix things with Kira.

Sami, Kira, and Kira's sister, Liv, watched as El rap-battled Darius King and proved that he was the real deal.

El didn't think he'd love anything as much as he loved sneakers—that is, until he found Kira.

the display. "This is amazing! This is the most beautiful thing I have ever seen!"

Kira laughed. She was enjoying El's reaction.

"This is my dream," he said. "My mom would have loved this." El looked at Kira. "So which ones are your favorite to wear?"

"Are you kidding?" she asked. "I'm not allowed to touch them, never mind wear them."

El slowed down when he spotted the OG Blues Darius King had worn in the NBA finals against the Celtics. He stopped and pointed to the classic sneakers.

"Not even once?" El asked Kira.

Kira hesitated and then leaned closer to El. "Okay. One time when I was a little kid, I wore them to the elevator, and then I chickened out and put them back."

El laughed and realized he couldn't take his eyes off Kira. He thought he would melt from her smile.

"Enough about my family," Kira said. She looked down at El's feet. "What kicks you rocking tonight?" As she stared at El's amazing sneakers, her eyes widened. "Oh my God," she whispered. "Did you design these?"

El nodded. Kira noticed the graffiti wall and clear soles with the tiny Queensboro Bridge inside. "Oh my gosh," Kira said. She reached out and shoved El. "You're him. You're *the* guy!"

"The . . . guy?" El asked.

Kira gushed on. "The guy with the secret celebrity collab. The guy everyone's been talking about tonight. My sister, Liv, has been going on and on about it." She couldn't believe El was the guy! She put her hand on his arm.

El was speechless. When Kira pressed him about being a designer and not telling her, he pushed back. "Manhattan, you didn't tell me you were Kira King," he said. "That is kinda an important thing to know. You are sneaker royalty!"

"Fair," she said. She curtsied in front of him. "Hi, I'm Kira King," she said, then extended her hand. "It's nice to meet you." She held on to his hand. "And listen, you have to come with me. It's destiny. Tonight is literally my last chance to prove to my dad there's a designer out there who is actually saying something and who has a point of view." She flashed him a smile. "And, El, you're him!"

El couldn't believe what he was hearing. Kira really

thought he was a famous sneaker designer. "You're saying I should design for the King brand?" he asked.

He wanted to shout, *No!* But he didn't want to disappoint Kira. He racked his brain for something to say. Before he could speak, he heard loud cheers from the party room.

Darius and Denise King were making their entrance to the gala. Kira heard her dad's voice booming over the sound system.

"That's him!" Kira cried, grabbing El's arm. "Come on!"

El followed her back into the party, wondering how he was going to get out of this situation.

CHAPTER
12

THE ROOM WAS EVEN MORE crowded now, and the large screens all showed the same image of Darius and Denise King. The couple stood center stage with grace and confidence.

Kira told El that when her dad was done with the welcome speech, she would introduce him. "He is gonna lose it when he sees your work," she said. She squeezed his hand tightly.

Liv was watching the speech from across the room. When Kira spotted her, she lost a little confidence—and her cool. "He will. I mean, it's kind of silly, but my dad, he says that experience really matters, and so he will want to know everything about you." Kira looked directly at El.

"Where you're from, what else you've done, who you've worked with . . ." Her voice trailed off.

"Who I've worked with?" El asked. He had a bad feeling.

"You're young, but the way you've blown up, you've obviously have had tons of professional gigs," Kira said. She smiled and added, "I got a lot riding on this." She looked over her shoulder at her parents.

The misunderstanding was getting bigger and bigger, and El's anxiety was intensifying. Kira took El's panic to be coyness about potential pending deals with Adidas or Nike. El didn't want to lie, but he also didn't want to let Kira down. She was looking at him with her brown eyes and her electric smile.

"I'm your guy," he said.

Kira hugged him. "I am never going to forget tonight," she said.

"Same," El managed to say, though his heart was beginning to race.

"Where have you been?" Liv said, glaring at Kira. She sidled up to her sister.

At the same moment, Sami appeared next to El. "Oh, good," she said. "You found her!"

"Hey, Sami!" Kira said enthusiastically.

Liv looked Sami and El up and down. "You know these people?" she asked.

"This is *the guy*, Liv!" Kira exclaimed.

"You're the guy?" Liv asked, looking at El.

Sami didn't let El answer. "Of course he's the guy. Look at his shoes," she said. She quickly changed the subject and asked Kira if she could take some photos of her. Sami pushed El closer to Kira. "Look at that power couple," she gushed, taking a bunch of pictures.

"I'm really excited," Kira said. "I want Dad to meet him. Isn't this exactly who you told me to find?" She turned to see her dad speaking to the crowd. "I wish he'd hurry up."

El heard Darius talking about honesty and integrity and how important these qualities were to him. He felt sick. How had he let this go so far?

Liv looked up at the clock. "It's almost midnight," she said. "You know he always starts the auction then."

El and Sami looked at each other. Midnight? Hadn't Gustavo said they had to be back by midnight?

GONG!

A bell rang the first stroke of the hour.

"Oh, no, we can't go," Sami said. "You're about to meet King."

"That's exactly the problem," El said. "I can't do it. I screwed up." Sweat began to form on his forehead, and his heart was racing full speed. His lie was catching up to him . . . and fast.

GONG!

"Sorry, I gotta get this guy outta here," Sami said. She took El's hand, and they bolted for the exit.

El turned back. "A curfew," he offered as his excuse, and disappeared into the crowd.

GONG!

The seconds were ticking by, and the hour chimes were making El and Sami move even faster.

"Wait!" Kira called. "You can't leave yet!" She raced after them.

GONG!

Liv was dumbfounded. "What is happening?" she asked, standing alone.

GONG!

El looked behind him to see Kira following. When he turned forward, he barreled right into a waiter holding a pitcher of water—and the water spilled all over him!

Sami ducked and then collided with a waiter balancing a tray lined with saucy appetizers. Food fell all over Sami.

GONG!

"Excuse me!" El called out as he scampered for the exit.

"Move!" Sami yelled to a crowd of people.

There was a buzz among the guests as El and Sami, soaked in water and sauce, pushed for the door. People—including Darius King—were beginning to notice the duo making a quick exit.

GONG!

El looked back at Kira. "I'm sorry! I have to go!" he shouted.

El jumped on the escalator and had to move quick as

he battled the upgoing steps. He bumped into someone and tumbled to the bottom. His foot caught the edge of a step, and his sneaker slipped off, stuck in the escalator, as he jumped off. He reached for the shoe, but it was already headed back up to the top.

Kira appeared and spotted a security guard near the top of the escalators. "Hey," she called to the guard. "Don't let him leave!" She pointed to El.

GONG!

El watched the sneaker make its way up the escalator.

Sami, already at the front door, was jumping around. "Leave it!" she screamed.

GONG!

Kira was standing at the top of the escalator. El caught her eye.

"El!" she called.

"Sorry," El said as Sami yanked him toward the large glass doors and out onto the street.

GONG!

El's sneaker made it to the top of the escalator and

stopped at Kira's foot. She reached down to pick it up. She held the shoe in her hand. El was gone, but at least she had his sneaker.

GONG!

El and Sami ran down the sidewalk and saw a tow truck pulling away with their orange car. On the windshield were a bunch of parking tickets.

"Noooooo!" Sami cried, running after the truck. "Wait!"

The truck sped around the corner, and then a car raced by, splashing water and mud all over them.

GONG!

Midnight.

El looked down at his wet, tattered clothes—and his one foot in its soggy sock without a sneaker. "Sami," he said, "why did everyone at the party think I was some hot underground designer who's blowing up worldwide?"

Sami kept walking.

"What did you say?" El demanded.

"Nothing!" Sami exclaimed. She stopped walking and

turned to face El. "Nothing . . . much," she said. "Just that you're a designer and you're, like, cool . . . and that's about it."

El gave Sami a hard stare. "Samantha," he said.

"Okay," she said with a shrug. "Maybe I hyped you up a little, but I barely said anything. I can't help what conclusions other people might have jumped to."

The two friends walked along the empty street.

"Kira asked me if I had professional experience," El said. He told Sami about how Kira wanted him to meet her father to talk about his shoe designs and how he'd lied about his experience.

Sami pumped her hand in the air. "That's amazing!"

"That's not good," El said as he continued to limp down the street in only one sneaker. "I lied to her."

"Look," she said. "Do you think anyone at that party was one hundred percent real? We both exaggerated a teeny amount, and it's gonna turn out great." She reached out to El and took his hand.

"How can I face her again after this?" El asked. They continued walking to the subway. There was no fancy car or special magic to take them back to Queens.

CHAPTER
13

THE NEXT MORNING, Kira and Liv kept watch for their dad to get up. They followed him into the elevator and down to the apartment lobby. "So tell me again, why did he run away?" Darius asked Kira.

After El's quick exit at the gala, Kira had to explain. She told her dad that El was a sensitive artist who got nervous and was likely intimidated by the idea of meeting an iconic sports figure. After all, King was a big deal. He would make anyone nervous.

Darius knew his daughter was buttering him up. He went to the front desk to pick up his messages. Kira handed El's sneaker to her dad.

"Look at the work," she said. "It speaks for itself."

"I admit," Darius said, examining the sneaker, "it does draw me in." He turned the shoe around. "I'm looking at something entirely new, but so familiar. It reminds me of home. I don't know why." He laughed when he saw the Greek bakery logo on the side. "I know that spot!" he exclaimed. "Your mom took me here when we first started dating." He tried to remember the name of their famous dessert.

Kira jumped in. "Galaktoboureko!" she said.

"Yes!" he said. Then he looked at Kira. "How'd you know that?"

"He took me there," she said.

Darius didn't like the fact that they didn't know anything about El's background, but he smiled at his daughter.

"He's worked with *plenty* of top-tier brands," Kira said. She knew the creative design was appealing to her dad. "Look how personal his work is. I trust him," she said. "I just really need you to trust me."

Her dad turned to Liv, whose eyes were on the sneaker. "I admit it's good work," she said. She paused, then voiced her concern. "The unknown factor just makes it very risky."

Kira held her breath as her dad turned to walk outside.

A black town car pulled up in front of the building. He handed the shoe back to Kira.

"Okay, Kira," he said. "Bring him in. If everything you say checks out, we'll try showcasing it at SneakerCon."

Kira jumped up and ran over to hug her dad. She danced up to the apartment. The plan had worked!

In her room, Kira stepped out onto her balcony, smiling as she looked at Queens. She was remembering the afternoon she'd spent with El.

Her thoughts were interrupted when Liv appeared at her door.

"I want you to understand how much is on the line for us right now," Liv said.

Kira stood straighter. She wasn't sure what her sister was going to say.

"Which is why I'll help you with anything you need, okay?" Liv said, a smile spreading across her face. "If this is what we're really doing, then let's do it. I'm all in."

Kira was glad she could count on her older sister for help. "Thank you! Now we just gotta find him," Kira said.

"Just call him," Liv said. "Text him."

When Kira confessed that she didn't know El's number, Liv scoffed. "Your game needs work." Liv softened a little when she saw her sister's face. Kira really liked the guy. And then Liv had an idea. There were forty million followers on the King Instagram account, and she was about to connect with them. "Let's do a whole King6 campaign to find the designer who has the match to the shoe."

The sisters began to make a plan.

Liv scrolled through images on her iPad. The lone shoe, the missing guy . . . she had the perfect slogan. Liv waited to see Kira's reaction.

Kira gave her approval, and Liv set off the plan for #WheresMyPrince.

Within the hour, Liv's campaign to find El was on.

Dressed in a silk black-and-gold outfit with an elegant updo weaved with gold ribbons, Kira sat on a throne with the solo sneaker on a regal tufted pillow. Touching the sneaker, Kira thought of how much work had gone into making the custom design. *Where are you?* she wondered.

A photographer started taking dozens of pictures of Kira on her throne as she held the single sneaker. Liv stood to the side, watching the shoot. It wasn't long before she felt they had the perfect shot.

Liv posted the photo on Instagram with the hashtag #WheresMyPrince. Within moments, she knew her idea was working. The post went viral. The media immediately picked up the story about the King sisters, who were flipping the script on Cinderella to find the sneaker designer.

More and more people saw the #WheresMyPrince post—and claimed to be the designer of the sneaker. There were plenty of guys ready to be the prince to Kira's princess. Kira and Liv invited the potential princes to the King store. A large crowd was already gathered. Guys were all trying to get Kira's attention by showing her their sneakers, but Kira was keeping her eye out for El. Why wasn't he answering the call? Didn't he know that the two of them could be a perfect fit?

At the end of the day, Kira went back to her apartment. She looked through the telescope on her terrace and focused on the graffiti wall in Queens. "Where are you?" she whispered.

CHAPTER
14

LATER THAT EVENING, in Astoria, El and Sami sat on a bench across the street from the graffiti wall.

"El, why didn't you show up today?" Sami asked. "You should have been there."

El didn't know what to say.

Sami put her phone in El's face. "You have seen this, right?" She flashed him a picture of Kira's #WheresMyPrince post. "A hundred million other people have," she said. "She put herself out there for you, so you gotta answer her."

El had seen the post. He shook his head.

"She digs your work," Sami said, grinning at him. "And from how hard she's trying to find you, I think that's not all she's into." She traced a heart with her fingers.

"This is really important to Kira," El said. "I don't want to hurt her."

Sami rolled her eyes. "Publicly ghosting someone is a great way *not* to hurt their feelings," she replied.

El wondered why Sami didn't understand. Kira believed El was someone important with design credentials. She wouldn't want to find out that he was a nobody who had never worked professionally. She wanted him to be something he wasn't. "You should have seen the relief on her face when she thought I was important," he said. He leaned back. "She doesn't want this, El."

"Don't talk about my best friend like that," Sami scolded him. She reminded him that Kira hadn't told them she was Kira King when they first met. "She doesn't care about that stuff," Sami said. She said she understood El was uncomfortable with what people had been led to believe about him at the gala, but as far as she was concerned, those stories weren't lies. Sami believed all those things were true. "But in order for the world to believe that," she said, "you gotta believe that first. Do you?"

El knew Sami was trying to help, but he couldn't shake

the feeling that he was an imposter. Then he closed his eyes and thought about Kira . . . and that electric smile.

Once El nodded his agreement, they sprang into action. The two best friends sprinted across the street and climbed up the ladder to the top of the shipping container where El and Kira had sat in front of the graffiti wall. He took his single gala-night sneaker out of his backpack and held it up in front of the frame Kira had spray-painted. Sami snapped a photo and then posted the picture on a new account, Sneaker Psychic. She typed in the tagline *Your match is right here and I'm ready to meet.* She put a lightning bolt emoji. And then she tagged Kira.

Sami knew it was only a matter of time before they heard from her. They walked slowly back to El's apartment to wait.

They didn't have to wait long.

"She DMed me," Sami said before they reached El's apartment. She stopped walking and stared at her phone.

El's heart stopped. *"And?"* he asked.

Before he could process what was happening, Sami had called Kira and tossed her phone to El.

Kira picked up!

El couldn't believe Kira was on the phone. He steadied his voice and tried to act cooler than he felt.

"Where have you been?" Kira asked.

"I was . . ." El trailed off. He looked at Sami for some support. She was dancing around, silently cheering him on. "I was being an idiot," El went on. "I was afraid, and I'm sorry. I'm sorry, but I'm done with that now."

Sami raised her thumbs up high. She grinned. El was finally being real with Kira.

"Are you sure?" Kira asked. "Listen, my dad's in, and he wants to set up a meeting, but if you run again, I'll—"

"I won't let you down," El told her.

"You promise?" Kira asked.

"Promise," El said.

Kira giggled. "Just checking."

El blushed as he said goodbye, filled with excitement.

As soon as the call ended, Sami and El started celebrating. They jumped around the street, cheering.

"El loves Kira King!" Sami sang out, dancing around. "El

and Kira King . . . ooooh! You're gonna design sneakers for her!"

They didn't realize that Stacy was upstairs in the apartment, watching them from the window.

CHAPTER 15

STACY REMEMBERED SEEING El and Sami by the graffiti wall on his way home. El had been posing with what looked like a sneaker, and now Sami was singing out Kira King's name? El was definitely planning something, and it was up to Stacy and Zelly to stop him, especially if his plan was going to jeopardize the sale of Laces and their way back to New Jersey.

Stacy dragged Zelly to the window to watch El and Sami out on the street. Though Zelly wasn't sure what El and Sami were up to, he listened to Stacy, who was urging him to teach El a lesson. They had to find proof that El was planning to ruin the Foot Locker deal.

The boys snuck into El's room, searching for clues.

They rifled through El's desk, opening drawers and going through papers.

Just then, the doorknob turned and the brothers slid under the bed to hide. El walked into his room to grab a drawing and left quickly, not seeing his stepbrothers. Stacy and Zelly followed El downstairs and spied him unlocking the secret workroom door. Stacy knew they had to get inside that room! Soon after, El went up to the apartment to shower. When El was in the shower, Zelly stuck his hand into the bathroom and took his key, which was hanging on a hook.

Stacy used the key to unlock the secret workroom and saw the gala sneaker sitting on the counter. "Oh," Stacy sighed. "This is what he's hiding!" He immediately recognized the shoe from the #WheresMyPrince post.

"Oh, that's a cool shoe!" Zelly exclaimed. He looked around. "Where's the other one?"

Stacy's eyes bugged out. How could his brother be so oblivious? "Get a clue," he spat. "Don't you get it? This is the proof!"

"But it's just a shoe?" Zelly asked innocently.

"Yeah," Stacy said. "Like the one in the news!" He was really going to lose his cool if Zelly didn't connect the dots. But he had to stay focused and think fast now that they had proof El was up to something. Stacy didn't have time to fully explain to Zelly. He told Zelly to throw boxes around the stockroom and make a mess.

"Wow," Stacy shouted at the foot of the steps to their apartment. "Look at this mess!"

"So messy," Zelly responded. "Ultra messy!"

El heard his brothers and walked down the stairs, then slipped on his work apron. He knew he would be blamed for the stockroom mess, so he started to clean up. While he was sweeping, Stacy snapped a picture of El.

The next morning, Stacy and Zelly turned off El's alarm so he would be late to his meeting with Darius King. They wanted to get to the office first to show Mr. King proof that El was just a stock boy from Queens—a fraud—and not some famous sneaker designer. With the shoe and the photograph, they took off early, ready to destroy El's plan.

CHAPTER 16

SAMI LOOKED AT HER PHONE and noted the time. "Let's roll, El," she said. "You're gonna be late."

El was scrambling. He had overslept and now was having a hard time deciding what to wear to the King meeting. Should he go professional with a tie, or not? He was debating with Sami as he opened the lock to his work space.

Sami followed El inside and picked up a few sketches for SneakerCon that were lying on the desk. She marveled at his original design, but El was focused on something else. His gala sneaker was missing! He had no idea that his stepbrothers had taken the shoe and that, at that moment, they were meeting with Darius King.

When El and Sami couldn't find the sneaker, Sami put El's sketches in a portfolio and handed them to him. "Kira knows you. She already knows you made that shoe. Just take your new design," she said. "I'm telling you, you bring this and you will win everybody over."

El hoped Sami was right. They made great time and were soon walking into the grand lobby of the King store.

"Kill it!" Sami said, giving El an elaborate handshake and then sending him up the massive escalators to the King offices.

El looked up and was shocked to see his stepbrothers riding the escalator down as he went up on the other side.

"It was really lovely meeting you," Stacy called to the top of the escalator. "Thank you for your time."

El was confused. What had his stepbrothers done?

"Good luck in your meeting," Stacy taunted El as they got near to him.

Zelly hit Stacy. "Don't we want the meeting to go bad?" he whispered.

Stacy rolled his eyes. He held up the photo of El cleaning the stockroom on his iPad as they passed El.

Now Darius would know he was just a stock boy. He would never believe El could design sneakers.

El saw Kira and Liv overlooking the escalator. Kira's face was stone cold. El knew he was probably too late, but he wanted a chance to explain to Darius—and to Kira.

"Kira," El began as he walked over to her.

"You wanted to meet with my father?" she said coldly. "Go ahead." She motioned for him to enter her dad's office.

El bravely walked into Darius's office. He tried not to be intimidated by the legend in front of him. Darius was standing behind his desk, and El immediately took in how tall the former NBA star was in person.

"Your brothers had a lot to say about you, El," Darius stated. He put El's sneakers on the desk.

El corrected him. "Stepbrothers," he said. El began to explain why Darius should not trust anything his stepbrothers had to say.

"Trust?" Kira asked, standing at the door. "You want to talk about trust?"

"Look, I can explain," El said, turning to face her.

Kira turned away. She couldn't even look at him.

Darius told El to have a seat. He called out El for lying to Kira. "Did you or did you not tell my daughter that you were a designer?" he bellowed. "A big-shot underground designer? With fans all over the world?"

"I . . . well, sort of," El sputtered. "I am a designer, but . . ."

Darius leaned forward with his large hands clasped together on the desk. "You lied," he said.

There was no way out of this. El had to come clean. "Yes," he said. He lowered his head, ashamed.

Darius accused El of using their social media to get more followers for himself. "This whole stunt was about you creating a name for yourself," he said. "You used our brand, our followers, to make some cash."

El felt heat in his face. "No," he said. "That's not—"

"It's not?" Darius said, cutting El off. "Is your father not in the middle of trying to off-load his failing store that's drowning in debt?"

"Stepfather," El clarified. "And it's my mother's store."

Darius sighed heavily and reached for the sneaker

sitting on his desk. "Did you even design this? Or was that a part of your hustle as well?" he asked.

Darius's words hung in the air.

El looked Darius in the eye. "No. I mean . . . yes, I did," he stammered. "That's all me. That shoe is everything."

"And we are supposed to believe you?" Darius asked. He shook his head and looked at Kira standing in the doorway. Her eyes were fixed on the ground.

"SneakerCon is in a couple weeks," Darius shouted, slamming down his hand on the desk. "You put us in a bind. My daughter vouched for you. She put herself on the line for the first time publicly. All for lies?" He pushed back in his chair, taking a deep breath. He gave El a long, cold look. "I think we're done here." He glanced at Kira as she walked away from the office. "Don't ever come around my daughter again." He stood up and turned his back to El.

The meeting was over.

El took his sketches and left the office. He called after Kira. He wanted to apologize to her, to explain his side of the story. He caught up to her in the hallway.

"How could you lie to me?" Kira asked. She was fighting back tears. "You knew what this meant to me."

El looked into Kira's eyes. He found some courage and spoke honestly. "You wanted me to be all those things that everyone said I was," he finally said.

"So this is my fault?" Kira snapped.

"No, of course not," El said. "I'm just saying my designs weren't enough for you." He took a deep breath. "I thought if I told you I was a stock boy, you wouldn't look at me the same." He stopped and waited for Kira's reply. "Look, I'm that same dude from that first day."

Kira felt tears welling up in her eyes and willed herself not to cry. "No, now you are just someone I never want to see again." She backed away. "Goodbye, El."

El's heart sank. "I'm sorry," he said. "Kira, I'm sorry." He wanted to race after her and get her to understand. He wanted to apologize again, but a security guard was escorting him out. He watched Kira disappear back into Darius's office.

El stepped on the escalator and slowly headed down to the large lobby. He found Sami waiting for him.

"Hey," Sami called out cheerfully. "How'd it go? We in business?"

"It's over," El said. He walked straight ahead to the subway, not saying another word. His heart ached. He shouldn't have lied to Kira, but he hadn't lied about his feelings. If only Kira knew how he felt . . .

Later that night, Kira walked out on her terrace, looking out toward Queens. Her heart was broken. Why had El lied to her? This whole mess could have been avoided if only he had been honest with her. He hadn't given her a chance. They could have been the best ever.

Kira went back into her room and sat down at her desk. She grabbed the rose El had given her from its vase and tossed the flower in the garbage.

CHAPTER
17

TREY'S DEAL WITH Foot Locker was going forward, and he posted GOING OUT OF BUSINESS signs around the store. El felt awful as he looked at the sales racks lined up. This was really happening. Laces was going to be taken over by Foot Locker, and there was nothing he could do.

He couldn't stop thinking of the meeting in Darius's office—and of Kira's face. He hated the way they'd left things. He walked to the back of the store and slipped into his work space. On the table was his sketch notebook, and he flipped through the pages. The designs were ideas for a new kind of sneaker he had been working on for Kira. El sighed and crumpled up the paper. Who was he kidding?

His design days were over. He spotted a gold *K* on the sketch that he had planned to weave into the fabric of the sneaker. He threw the crumpled design in the trash.

El took the trash can out to the dumpsters in the alley behind the store. Mrs. Singh was trying to lift her garbage can into a large dumpster. El rushed over to help her. "Mrs. Singh," he said, "you know I always grab these on Wednesday night."

"I'm gonna have to get used to doing it myself," she said.

Mrs. Singh saw El's face. She knew how El felt about the store being sold and the move. She tried to make him feel better. "It's okay. It will be my cardio," she said with a smile. "I really can't believe you're leaving, honey. It all happened so quickly. Stay in touch."

"I'm really gonna miss you," El said, hugging her tightly.

El went back inside to his empty room, already packed up for the move in the morning. He sat on the ledge in front of his window, looking out toward Manhattan. He wondered what Kira was doing right then.

The wind blew hard and picked up the crumpled sneaker design El had thrown in the dumpster. The paper was lifted off the ground and swirled around. It bounced along the pavement until it landed at the gate of the community gardens. Gustavo picked up the paper and carefully smoothed out the sheet, examining El's sneaker design.

Gustavo shook his head.

What would become of El's dream? Would he never see his passion and talent fulfilled because of one mistake? Or would the neighbor El loved and the spirit he represented come together to give him one more chance?

He smiled.

That would be its own kind of magic.

CHAPTER 18

KIRA WAS JUST WAKING UP when her mom poked her head inside her room.

"Hey, today's the big day. It's game day!" Denise said brightly. She was surprised to find Kira still in bed.

"For Liv," Kira said sadly. She didn't want to go to SneakerCon and see her sister's designer get all the attention. She knew she had messed up.

"No, for all of us," her mom said. "You're a big part of this company, too, Kira." She sat down on Kira's bed. "And this family. We're all Kings."

Kira sighed. "I don't feel like one," she said.

"Well, you gotta straighten your crown," her mom told

her. "You know," Denise went on, "I've been really proud of you these past few weeks."

Kira shook her head. "Why? I screwed up big-time," she said. "It was all a lie," she added in a whisper.

"All?" her mom asked. "That boy clearly got in over his head. But then again, so did you."

Kira sat up. "How is it my fault he lied?" she snapped. "I don't understand."

Denise reached out and moved some hair away from Kira's face. "I suppose it's impossible you wanted this so badly that you might have led him into saying what you needed to hear?"

Kira knew her mom was right—as hard as it was for her to hear. She paused and let her words sink in.

"Listen to me," her mom said. "It's not easy as a young woman to stand up and have your voice heard above everybody else's—especially your father's."

Kira knew that was true.

"But you did," her mom said, smiling. "And I'm very proud of you for that. Because that means you are starting to find your own voice and trust yourself." She grinned at her daughter. "That means you are growing up."

Kira appreciated her mom's saying all that, but it didn't change the fact that she had messed up. Denise encouraged her to move forward.

"The important thing is that you figure out what you can do differently next time," her mom said.

Kira nodded. "Yeah, I guess you're right."

"Oh, of course I am!" her mom exclaimed. She hitched her head back and laughed loudly. "Baby, you know how many of these talks I've given over the years? To Liv, to your dad . . ." She smiled at Kira and took her hand. "He didn't become 'the King' on his own, my love."

Kira laughed along with her mom. It felt good to laugh. She felt better already.

Their laughter brought Liv—still in her pajamas, with bed hair sticking up all over—to Kira's door.

"What's so funny?" Liv asked, rubbing her eyes.

That only made Kira and her mom laugh more.

"You talking about me?" Liv asked.

Kira and her mom laughed as Denise ushered Liv out of the room. They all had to get ready for SneakerCon. The Kings were due to make an appearance soon.

♔

El's phone was buzzing, and he opened one eye to turn off his alarm. When the alarm sounded again, he looked at his phone. Rubbing his eyes, El glanced at the banner across the top, which alerted him that SneakerCon was happening that day. He hit snooze again. He didn't want anything to do with SneakerCon.

It was moving day. He didn't need to wake up early for that, so he tried to get back to sleep.

The third time the alarm went off, El opened his eyes a little wider. All his boxes were packed up and stacked in his room, but he saw something on the windowsill. He sat up.

Was he dreaming?

He got up from the bed and went to the window. He couldn't believe what he was seeing. The pair of sneakers he had sketched for Kira was sitting on the windowsill. They were real! Even the golden *K* he had envisioned was stitched perfectly on the side.

His phone alarm sounded again, with the banner across the top blinking *SneakerCon*. He tried to turn off the alarm, but the sound wouldn't stop.

"I gotta go," he said.

El put the sneakers in his backpack and stuck his head out his bedroom window. He spotted Stacy and Zelly loading the moving truck on the side of the store. Farther up the street, El saw Sami heading to the store on her skateboard. El opened the window wider and leaned out, motioning Sami to stop. He pointed to his stepbrothers.

"I need you to stall them," El called down to Sami when the boys went inside. "I gotta get to SneakerCon."

Sami's face lit up. "You're going?" She jumped up and down. "Yes!"

"I gotta find Kira and make things right," he said. "I got kicks to deliver."

"I'm so proud of you," Sami said, getting emotional.

El smiled. "Do what you do best and make a scene!" he told her.

"Say no more," Sami said, grinning. "I got you!"

Sami made a nuisance of herself to distract Stacy and

Zelly. She jumped up on the moving truck and took out Zelly's judo gear. She put on his jacket and then grabbed Stacy's prized debate trophy. As the boys were struggling to get their stuff back, El slipped out the back door, unnoticed, and headed to SneakerCon.

CHAPTER 19

AT THE KING STORE, a camera crew was setting up for the livestream that would start SneakerCon. The feed would stream to the convention center in Cleveland, Ohio, where thousands of sneaker fans were waiting for the King announcement. Everyone was talking about King's newest sneaker and eagerly awaiting the presentation.

For the big broadcast, large monitors were spread around the store to capture the hundreds of fans lined up outside, and they also showed the convention center in Ohio. The hype was hot!

Kira stood off to the side as Liv gave a teaser to the sneaker announcement. Holding a microphone and looking at the camera, Liv spoke to the fans in Cleveland and outside the store.

"We are so excited to be broadcasting directly to our fans at SneakerCon today," Liv said, smiling into the camera. "We have a special treat lined up that you will not want to miss, so be sure to watch live at ten a.m." The crowd roared with excitement. "And thanks to all our amazing supporters who turned up this morning! We love you!"

Kira glanced up at the monitors. The television news cameras outside were picking up the faces of the fans waiting and cheering. As Kira turned away, she missed the camera focusing on El. He was right in front of the store.

Back in Astoria, Stacy spotted El on Mrs. Singh's television in her storefront window. Stacy rushed over to Zelly. At first Zelly didn't understand the emergency, but then Stacy explained that El's being at the King store while SneakerCon was going on could ruin their plan of returning to New Jersey.

"El is gone," Stacy said. "He's gone to some SneakerCon thing at King6's. What if he can get enough money to keep the store?"

"Should we go there?" Zelly asked. "I can drive."

Stacy grabbed the keys from his brother and slid into the driver's seat of the truck.

"Dad!" Stacy cried when Trey walked out of the store. "El took off, but we know where he is. We'll meet you at the new house in an hour!"

"Wait!" Trey screamed. "Where are you going?" He stood in the middle of the street as Stacy drove the truck away. "Come back here!" He picked up one of the crushed traffic cones the truck had run over. "I cannot afford this!" he said. He turned and saw Sami. "What is going on? Can you just tell me where El is?"

Sami walked over to Trey but didn't answer.

"I can't deal with him trying to sabotage anything to do with this deal," Trey said. "I know he doesn't want to leave, but he just doesn't get it."

Sami shook her head. She had to get real with Trey. "*You're* the one who doesn't get it," she said. "Your stepson is talented and kind and hopeful, despite all your best efforts." She took a deep breath. She had to be honest. "You know what? I think it's time you see El for who he really is."

CHAPTER 20

THE EXCITEMENT WAS BUILDING as the live broadcast for SneakerCon got closer.

"It's the moment you've been waiting for," the announcer sang out. "Put your hands together for the MVP, four-time NBA champion Darius King!"

Music blared from the speakers, and dancers lined up on the stage.

"Can we give it up for the King?" the announcer asked. "Let's get nineties, SneakerCon!"

The crowd cheered as the dancers parted and Darius started his old-school nineties rap. He was wearing a vintage basketball uniform from when he'd been a star player.

Kira looked at the screens around the store to witness the crowd's reaction. There were so many people outside cheering for her dad. This time when the camera landed on El, Kira saw him. She did a double take. Then she spotted him through one of the large store windows. El held up a shoebox and gestured for her to move to the entrance.

Kira made her way to the front door, but El was stopped by security.

"Kira!" he called.

Kira waved away security. "What, El?"

He held out the box. "These are for you," he called to her. "Please take them. I'll leave right after."

Kira hesitated, but she took the box. She lifted the lid. The sneakers took her breath away. She took out one of them and examined the details. A smile spread across her face. "They even have a *K* on them," she said. "Is that for me?"

"They are one of ones," he said. "Just like you." He took a moment to gather his courage. "I know I lied to you, but that is not who I am. I'm the son of Rosie Morales, a magical, amazing woman who taught me sneakers could be a window into someone's soul and that they can show you someone's experiences and tell you who someone is and what they care about." He stopped for a moment and looked into Kira's eyes. "I'm sorry it took me so long to say that," he said. "All I care about . . . is you."

Kira looked up at El. "It's too late, El," she said. "We already have the kick we're dropping today."

"You think I came here for that?" El asked. "I came here to say I'm sorry."

Before Kira could react to El's speech, Liv stormed up to them. She pushed El back. "You? Out!" Liv spat. "You've done enough damage around here already. You completely embarrassed my family and hurt my sister."

Kira put her hand on Liv's arm. "Liv, it's okay," she said. "El came here to apologize. And so should I."

El hadn't expected Kira to say that. "What are you talking about?" he asked.

"I'm really sorry that I pushed you to say all that stuff. My dad, he said that experience mattered, and I got so wrapped up in that. I forgot what really matters—what I want my family to stand for, and what I believe in. Your talent, your passion. El, you are amazing, and I believe in you. And that should be enough."

She showed Liv the sneakers El had designed. "Kinda spectacular, huh?"

Liv backed down. She could see that the sneaker was unique and special. "I'm not the one you have to convince," she said, shrugging. She looked over her shoulder at Darius. "You clearly put your voice in your work," she said. "Can you bring it to the stage?" She handed El the microphone.

Kira smiled. "El, you got this."

"For you, Manhattan," El said, taking the microphone, "anything."

As El approached the stage, Darius looked surprised. "You again?" he asked.

El wanted to be honest with Darius, and now he had a grand audience. Darius wasn't easily swayed, but he listened. El rapped his explanation. He smoothly rhymed about how he was a kid from Queens, like Darius. He, too, was a kid with big dreams. El handed Darius the sneaker he had made for Kira.

Immediately, Darius was taken with the original design

of the shoe. He held up the sneaker for all to see just as Stacy and Zelly barreled through the crowd.

"No!" Stacy shouted. "Stop!"

Trey and Sami arrived just as Stacy and Zelly took the stage. The twins tried to convince Darius and the crowd that El was a fraud.

"Zelly? Stacy?" Trey called. He was surprised to see his sons there. "What is going on?"

Darius moved over to Trey. He introduced himself and called Trey out on how he had been dealing with the feud between the boys, and how he had been treating El. "Talent gets you where you want to be," he said, tossing one of El's sneakers to him.

Trey examined the shoe. He confessed that he hadn't understood El before, but El had never shown Trey his work. He wanted to be a better man and hoped El would give him a second chance.

"Everyone deserves a second chance," El told him. He reached out, and the two embraced tightly.

Darius was smiling. He, too, had decided to give El a second chance. And more than that, he wanted to make El an offer to be a partner with him for a new sneaker line. He watched El's reaction to the news. Then he gave El an opportunity to come clean with any other secrets.

El did have one other secret he was eager to share. He looked at Kira. "I'm in love with your daughter," he said.

The crowd went wild. Kira's face broke into a wide smile.

She was very happy to hear El's confession. Even Darius had to smile.

One year later, El was living in Astoria and helping out Gustavo in the community gardens. The flowers were blooming beautifully, and El picked a bunch of roses from Rosie's patch. He took the bouquet of flowers back to Kira, who was waiting for him on the corner. Kira was comfortable in Astoria now. Together, El and Kira had transformed Laces into a new space. The shop was now El's own sneaker studio and store. His deal with Darius was to create a new line of sneakers, and he and Kira had developed a brand called El-evate. His dream of designing sneakers had come true.

Sami was the El-evate publicist. She was thrilled to

promote the brand and take photos of the many fans waiting to get inside the store. People lined up around the block to get in and to buy the newest sneaker.

Life is what you make it, El thought happily as he looked around the store. He watched customers wearing his sneakers and carrying El-evate bags. He hoped his sneakers would lift people up and inspire them.

He smiled at Kira, glad that she was at his side. Finally, he was doing what he was meant to do, and the store was back in the sneaker business. He knew his mother would be proud.

He and Kira had created a brand of sneakers that were meant to make people soar.

And so goes the story of a boy who tried to soar in the king's shoes but ultimately found the best way to take flight was to stay true to his roots—and maybe give a little lift to the next dream.